THERE'S A BEAR ON MY CHAIR

ROSS COLLINS

nosy crow

There's a bear
on
my
chair.

He is so big
it's hard to share.
There isn't any
room to spare.

We do not
make a happy pair,
a mouse and bear
with just one chair.

When I give him
a nasty glare,
he seems completely
unaware.

I don't know
what he's doing there,
that bear who's sitting
on my chair.

I must admit he has
some flair.
He has fine taste
in leisurewear.
I'm fond of how
he does his hair.

But still I wish he
was not there.

I'll try to tempt him with a pear,
to **lure** him from my favourite chair.

But he just leaves it
sitting there.
Why **won't** he
go back
to his lair?

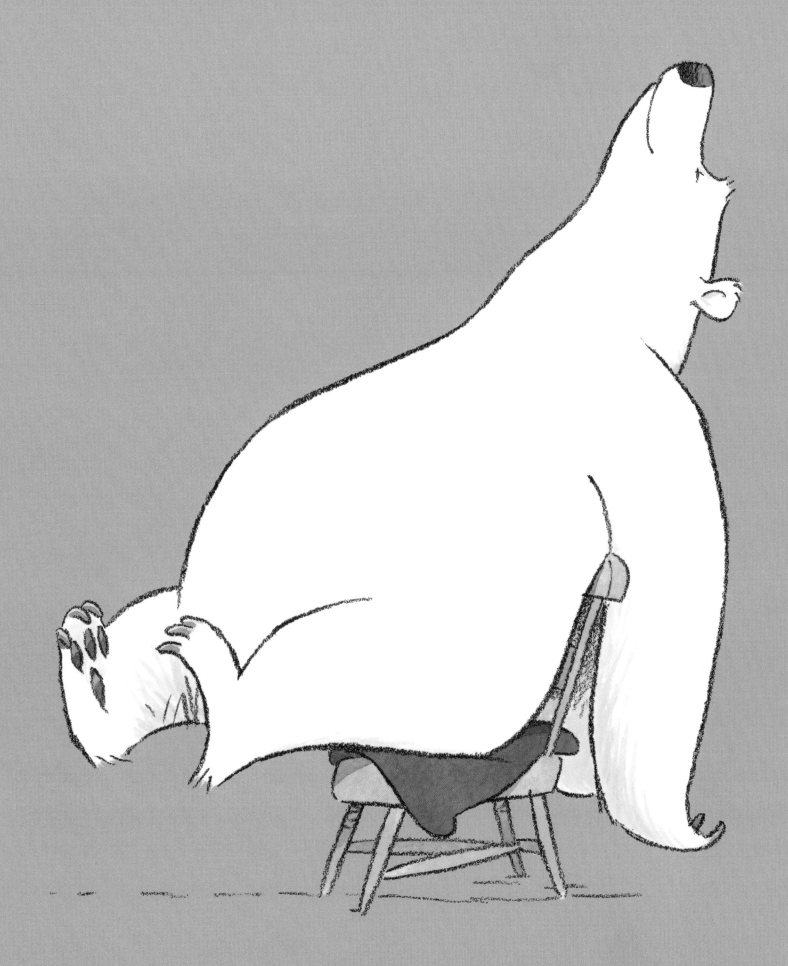

Perhaps if I give
him a **scare** . . .

I'll **jump** out
in my **underwear!**

But **no.**
Of course,
he does not care.

That stinky bear
sat on my chair.

I understand that bears are rare.

I know they need the utmost care.

I know all that.

I am aware.

But still

I cannot

stand

this

bear.

That's it! I'm done!
I do declare!
This bear
has led me to
despair!

It is not fair!

It is not fair!

I'm going now.
I don't know where . . .

Hey!

There's a mouse
in my house.